# Daisy the Daydreamer

## An Adventure with Dinosaurs

Written by Keiara Robinson
Illustrated by Amariah Rauscher

Daisy the Daydreamer: An Adventure with Dinosaurs
Copyright ©2019 by Keiara Robinson
Illustrations ©2019 by Amariah Rauscher

Printed in the United States of America by Keiara Robinson

ISBN-10: 1-6763-8906-7
ISBN-13: 978-1-6763-8906-4

The text of this book is set in 14 pt Minion Pro font.
The illustrations in this book were created using watercolor and charcoal.

## Dedication

To my younger self, let your imagination run wild.

Daisy Sullivan has a very active imagination. She absolutely loves school and learning new subjects. All of her teachers adore her, but they also know how much she enjoys daydreaming. Daisy just can't help herself! Once engulfed in a new lesson, her mind begins to run wild.

Today, we find Daisy in Mrs. Pepperdine's class learning about . . . dinosaurs! Daisy's eyes fill with excitement and anticipation as Mrs. Pepperdine begins to speak, "Dinosaurs existed more than two hundred million years ago..."

In an instant, Daisy's mind skips out of the classroom and she begins to imagine what it must have been like to live among dinosaurs. She soon finds herself in a wooded area surrounded by large trees. The air is crisp and the sun is hot.

Suddenly, she hears a loud screech overhead. She can't make out what it is, but the leaves on the trees shake violently as it passes by.

Daisy runs through the dense brush eager to see what made such a sound. As she makes her way through the woods, the scenery begins to change and she is now standing on a rugged, dirt terrain.

Daisy squints up at the sky and finally sees it, a Pterodactyl soaring above her. She is in awe of the flying reptile and calls out to the creature as best she can, "Caw, Caw." The animal swoops down and plunges into the nearby lake to help itself to some fish. After all, Pterodactyls are carnivores, Daisy surmises.

She makes her way along the terrain anxious to see what other dinosaurs she will encounter. Daisy comes across some baby Triceratops ferociously ripping into the grass with their beaks. She was unaware that this breed of dinosaur was an herbivore. At that moment, the ground beneath her begins to tremble.

Daisy sees large patches of dust swirling in the distance and hears the faint sound of a stampede getting closer and closer. The mother Triceratops calls out to her young, and they quickly disappear into the woods. Daisy hurries to hide behind a bush, and it's just in the nick of time!

A herd of Brachiosaurus make their way past Daisy. She holds onto the branches of the bush as the earth continues to quake.

Once Daisy believes she is in the clear, she lifts her head above the shrub only to see a Tyrannosaurus Rex charging full speed towards her. Daisy is immediately paralyzed with fear. She then becomes a bit perplexed, not because of the imminent danger headed her way, but because the large beast seems to be yelling her name, "Daisy! Daisy!"

How odd she ponders, this dinosaur sounds a lot like . . . uh oh, Mrs. Pepperdine! "Miss Daisy Sullivan, where have I lost you to this time?" Mrs. Pepperdine asks.

Daisy quickly answers, "I was just getting a little more acquainted with our prehistoric friends."

"Oh, really," says Mrs. Pepperdine, "and which of these 'prehistoric' friends of yours is a herbivore, Miss Sullivan?"

Daisy recalls the little Triceratops eating the grass in her daydream and answers confidently, "The Triceratops!" Mrs. Pepperdine gives her a stern look with a slight smile growing across her face. The bell rings, and it is time for Daisy's favorite part of the school day -- recess!

Daisy joins her best friend, William Cheng, by the jungle gym; another of Daisy's favorites! Daisy begins to tell William all about her adventure with the dinosaurs while daydreaming in Mrs. Pepperdine's class. William loves to hear about Daisy's adventures and sometimes they go on these adventures together. Today seems to be one of those days!

As they race each other to the top of the jungle gym, they find themselves overlooking the prehistoric world Daisy envisioned earlier in class. This time Daisy is with William high above the woods at the top of one of the tallest trees.

Daisy points down and says, "Look!"

William can barely see the baby Triceratops below near the lake. Excited and astonished, he shouts, "Cool!"

Daisy then points up to the sky to her reptile friend soaring in the distance. "What's that?" William asks.

"That's a Pterodactyl," Daisy replies.

The creature perches on a nearby tree branch.

"Whoa," giggle Daisy and William as the surrounding branches bow and bounce.

The animal seems to call out to them.

"I think it wants us to go with it," says Daisy.

"I'm not so sure. Is it safe?" questions William.

"Let's find out," yells Daisy, as she makes her way across the branches in the direction of the prehistoric bird. As they settle onto the Pterodactyl's neck, it immediately takes off in flight! Daisy and William hold on tight as the wind begins to whip past their faces and everything below them becomes smaller and smaller.

The two are having a blast! Daisy and William laugh and smile as they fly through the air. The Pterodactyl then makes a perfect landing by the lake, and they dismount. Daisy and William thank their new friend and wave goodbye as the creature departs giving out one last screech, as if to say, "You're welcome!"

They quickly turn to the lake and playfully splash each other. Unexpectedly, a huge head surfaces from beneath the water startling both Daisy and William. They fall backwards landing on the dirt behind them and looking up they see a Plesiosaurs emerge. The large dinosaur is lazily chewing on some seaweed completely unaffected by their presence.

"That's a herbivore. They only eat greens," Daisy explains as William nods his head in agreement.

Again, the earth starts to shake. William turns to Daisy with his eyes wide and his mouth open in shock. "Run," Daisy yells. "It's a Tyrannosaurus Rex…and they are carnivores."
"What does that mean?" yells back William, as they take off!

"They eat meat!" cries Daisy.

To add to the unwanted surprise, a group of Saltopus run ahead of the T-Rex and one of the rather little dinosaurs jumps up and nips at Daisy's jeans.

She screams just as a soccer ball hits her leg and is relieved to find themselves in the middle of the school's soccer field where her classmates are playing.

"Move it!" one of the kids shouts.

Daisy and William lower their heads, apologize, and run off the field.

"That was awesome," William says out of breath as he nudges Daisy.

"Yea," she responds with flushed cheeks as the bell rings bringing recess to an end.

Daisy spends the remainder of the day anxiously awaiting the end of school and dismissal. It's Friday, which means her mother will be picking her up from school today. Finally, the last bell rings! Daisy jumps up out of her seat, grabs her book bag, and heads for the door. She sees her mother waving from the sidewalk and runs straight into her mother's arms.

"How was your day?" her mother asks.

"Great," says Daisy.

"Good, you can tell me and your father all about it once we get home," her mother replies. Daisy can barely control her enthusiasm as she and her mother get into the car and head home. Daisy loves to come home and tell her parents about her adventures, whether they believe her or not!

As soon as they get home, Daisy heads to her room to complete her homework assignments. Her mother calls out to her, "I'll let you know when dinner is ready. Your father should be home shortly."

As Daisy finishes up her multiplication tables, her mother yells, "Dinner's ready!"
She immediately puts down her pencil and paper and begins to cheerfully skip downstairs.

Upon reaching the bottom of the stairs, the front door opens. "Daddy's home," Daisy sings and is lifted up by her father for a big hug. He gives her a kiss on the cheek and they head to the dining room. Daisy's day is finally complete, sitting at the dinner table with her parents, and chatting about her marvelous explorations…another of her many favorites!

Her father asks, "How was school today, baby girl?"

"Well," begins Daisy, "I learned about dinosaurs in Mrs. Pepperdine's class." Knowing she now has her parent's attention, Daisy continues, "I actually flew on a Pterodactyl, came face to face with a Plesiosaurs, and was chased by a Tyrannosaurus Rex!"

Daisy's parents look at her inquisitively.

"It's true, I really did! I hung out with all types of dinosaurs today, both herbivores and carnivores. I swear, William was there too," she explains.

"Wow, seems like you had quite an active day today! Better eat up," says her father.

Once dinner is finished, Daisy is excused from the table and heads upstairs to get ready for bed. Her father tells her that he will be up shortly to help with her homework, and her mother sends her off with a kiss on the forehead.

As her mother is clearing the table, she catches a glimpse of Daisy's shorts. There is a slight rip on her right back jean pocket. She points this out to her husband. They look at each other in disbelief, but then laugh it off; both thinking it couldn't be…or could it!

# About the Author

Keiara Robinson is the up-and-coming author of a new book series called *Daisy the Daydreamer*. Having had the idea as a young girl, Keiara is thrilled to finally bring Daisy Sullivan to life, a character destined to break barriers and take on the world! Growing up, Keiara rarely saw other children that resembled her. As a biracial woman, she is proud to present a story line that promotes diversity. Keiara has always had a love of writing. Her mother taught her at a young age the necessity of a good vocabulary, which shines through in her current work. Keiara encourages early readers to explore new words in order to improve their communication skills because words have power.

Find Daisy on the web:
www.daisythedaydreamer.com
IG: @daisythedaydreamer
Facebook: @daisythedaydreamer

Made in the USA
Monee, IL
19 January 2020